Jitters

By Ken Stark

Keep making a face like that, Harold, and one day it'll stick!

The man lay naked on the bed, sneering up at the ceiling as his mother's needling voice played back in his head. The fact that she'd been right all along didn't even rate consideration. After all, who or what in this whole goddammed world deserved any better than a sneer? Those mindless trolls on the bus? The dick of a boss who couldn't wait to dump all over him? The dried up old buzzard in Human Resources with the turned-up nose and the claw full of pink slips? *Christ*, who or what in this whole toilet of a world deserved anything better than a sneer? They should all just consider themselves damn lucky that the sneer didn't come with a side order of Smith and Wesson.

The imagery only widened his sneer.

What he wouldn't give to pay back those vindictive pricks. And maybe he would, one day. Yessir, maybe he would do just that! He'd never held a gun in his life, but how hard could it be? Pull the trigger and watch that ol' smoke-wagon jump. And then again, and again, and again. Pull that trigger and keep on pulling, and show those dicks who was boss, one by one by one by everlovin' one.

Dammit, it wasn't fair! They'd all conspired against him, and now he was right back where he'd started. And didn't that just show exactly how this world worked? He'd moved away ten years ago, all full of piss and vinegar, ready to make his way in the world, and how had the world repaid him? With a resounding kick in the balls, that's how. And now he was back. At the ripe old age of thirty, he was right back where he'd started. All the way back to square one.

Well, yippee-*fuckin'*-yahoo.

She hadn't said it yet, but he knew his mother would eventually offer some homespun bit of wisdom about the whole situation, and sure as shit, she'd find a way to pin it all on him. She'd never met his boss, never saw the trolls on the bus, had no idea what kind of Hell he had to endure day in and day out, but she'd make it his fault, same as always. The woman couldn't cook a proper meal or clean a house to save her life, but *goddam* if she couldn't emasculate a man at the drop of a hat.

Christ! A man of thirty shouldn't be in this situation. A man of thirty should be in his own house where he could walk around in his underwear if he was of a mind. A man of thirty should have a wife cooking dinner and cleaning up after her man and pouring him a beer after a hard day's work. A man of thirty should have two or three snot-nosed kids running around so he could tell them to take out the garbage and mow the lawn, and when they didn't get straight A's in school, he could tell them how stupid they were and that they'd never amount to anything. That was how things were supposed to work. Circle of life, baby. Circle of mother-fucking life.

His grimace deepened into a scowl.

Hell, a man of thirty should own a house. In fact, a man of thirty should own *this* house! A man of friggin' thirty should have bought the mortgage right out from under the noses of those two walking corpses so that the'd have had to come to him on their knees instead of the other way around. *Please let us live here, sir....* they'd have to beg, *Please, oh please let us stay here, just until we get back on our feet....* Oh, and wouldn't it had given him a world of happy to have looked those two old farts right in their puffy grey faces and hurl a big fat NO! right down their open, toothless mouth. Yesiree, doctor, that would have given him a whole goddam *world* of happy!

A mean little smile crept across his scowl as he hauled himself upright, but it turned back into a sneer as his bare feet hit the floor. The thick pile carpeting was probably meant to be soft and luxurious, but he'd never thought of it that way. It was the colour of snot, and deep enough that anything at all might be crawling around down there, laying their eggs and dropping their shit. For all he was worth, every single step he'd ever taken across that snot-yellow carpet made him feel like he was wading through a cesspool. And after a dozen years with him out in the world getting his balls kicked, who the hell knew what was down there?

He threw a silent curse at the world in general and stood up, scratching an itch on his backside and bringing his fingers up to his nose for a quick sniff.

The room was smaller than it'd been when he was a boy, and that was saying a lot. Before, it had been dungeon, now it was a closet, complete with the stink of age. Well, maybe it wasn't just the room that'd changed in size, he had to admit, drawing a hand across his protruding belly, but what the hell. So what if he'd put on a few pounds? So what if he had to drop by the Sally-Ann every few weeks for a new pair of jeans that didn't make his fat bunch up and spill out over the top like a blueberry muffin. It had been a rough bunch of years, and he deserved every Ding Dong and every bag of Doritos he'd scarfed down along the way.

Two years. Two lousy years he'd spent in that dung-pit of a job. It was the longest he'd ever stayed in one place, and how had those dickwads thanked him for hanging on for so long? By yanking his livelihood right out from under his feet, that's how. No job, no money. No money, no pad. No pad, no chicks. Okay, well the 'chicks' were always more imaginary than real, but dammit, the potential was always there! At least until those assholes flushed his entire life right down the toilet.

"Goddamn assholes!" he swore aloud as he waddled across the room to the window, satisfying an itch under one arm and giving his fingers another sniff.

It took fewer steps to get to the window than he'd remembered, but the view was exactly the same. Whoever'd built the place back in the dark ages had cut a little square hole in the ground and stuck in a dirty little pane of so-old-it-had-begun-to-ripple glass so they could call it 'natural light' and squeeze a few more bucks out of his idiot parents. And it worked, because what did *they* care? The old man would never set foot down here, and the old lady only made the trip once in a blue moon to throw in a load of laundry. What did they care if their one and only child lived in a tomb?

On the best day, a tiny sliver of light might happen to squeeze through, but just barely, and only when the sun was high in the sky. Even standing on tip-toe and craning his fat neck as far up as he possibly could, all he could see now was dirt and crabgrass.The foundations of the house were thick, so the window itself was set back a foot, and so high that it was completely out of reach. When he was younger and thinner, he would sometimes grab hold of the sill and pull himself up like chinning a bar, but even when he'd managed to turn the hasp and push the window open as far as it would go, not a breath of air even came through. And so he'd stopped trying. He'd left it open twelve years ago, and open it still was, and he doubted whether a single molecule of fresh air had found its way through in all that time.

"Goddamn Alcatraz....." he sneered up at the window.

He returned to bed with a scowl, perched himself on the foot of the sagging mattress, and reached for his pack of cigarettes atop a rickety little table against the wall. That damned table had stood in the exact same spot since he was a kid, ever since his mother brought it home with declarations of making it their 'special project'. Together, they'd strip the paint, fix that one leg that was an inch shorter than the others, and try their hand at some sort of art-nouveau, marble-ass painting some guy on TV swore would make even the oldest, crappiest piece of derelict furniture look like something out of Buckingham Palace. But the two of them had never gotten around to that 'special project', had they? And now, fifteen years later, the paint was still the colour of pus, and the goddam thing rocked and swayed like a drunk at the slightest touch.

Just you wait and see, Harold...., he heard her say in his head, *Just you wait and see how good this table looks when we're through....*

He'd stopped believing in fairy tales by then, so as he grabbed up the half-empty pack of smokes and watched the table cant to the side, he allowed a self-satisfied snort at his own foresight. He knew they'd never get around to their special project in a month of

Sundays, and just like always, he'd been proven right. Yeah, okay, he'd always managed to find something better to do whenever the subject came up, but what kid wanted to spend a day stripping paint with his mother when there were so many good shows on TV?

He drew out a smoke and tossed the rest of the pack onto the table, and sneered again as it rocked and swayed in protest. He flicked a lighter and sucked in a deep lungful of smoke, then he flipped the lighter onto the table and snorted a double-stream through his nose as the table swayed one more time.

Just you wait and see, Harold.....

Yeah, right.

He glanced at his wristwatch and sighed. Eight o'clock on a Friday night. He should be out on the town right this very moment, yet here he was, locked up in his own private Hell while the old fogeys who were out having fun. Well, pinochle at the Henderson's couldn't exactly be considered 'fun' by any stretch of the imagination, but they were still out, weren't they? And they were sure as shit having a more enjoyable evening than yours truly. Even putting up with old Wilt Henderson's cheating and cigar-puffing and spending the time between plays regaling the troops with his tales of daring-do back in 'Nam had to be better than sitting around in a Sandinista jail cell scratching your balls.

He collapsed onto his back and rubbed his oversized belly, poking idly at the little cache of lint in his navel, then he lifted a butt cheek and farted his contempt at the whole world.

"Goddam Alcatraz," he said again, sneering up at the empty house.

Just then, the sound of a car's engine broke the silence, and for one horrible moment, he thought that the card game must have broken up early. But no. Not with that rusted-out muffler. That could only be Jimmy Stanton, next door. The old coot ran on a schedule tighter than a nun's ass. Out of the house at 9:47 sharp to be at the Pharmadeal for opening at 10:00 o'clock, and pulling the old Valiant back into the garage precisely at 8:13. He'd never said two words to the man, so he couldn't imagine what the old geezer did before, during or after, but of two things he was certain; out at 9:47, and back at 8:13. Sharp. Every single day. Every single mother-fucking day since the beginning of time.

He looked again to his watch and read it as three minutes after, taking the time to recognize that the watch was ten minutes slow but not bothering to reset it, and registering no irony whatsoever in thinking that doing so would be a waste of his valuable time.

8:13.

He rolled the numbers around in his mind with all the enthusiasm of a cold bowl of oatmeal. 8:13 on a Friday night. Dammit, Friday nights were made for partying! Partying and drinking and hoping that the fat little thing across the way couldn't hold her alcohol and had a low enough self-esteem to partake in a little slap and tickle in the parking lot. God didn't create Friday nights for sitting along in a hot-as-Hell jail cell pulling your pud all by your lonesome. Hell, no! Friday nights were made for loud music and smoke as thick as fog and finding some sad little thing willing to pull your pud *for* you. Someone young and sweet and with long hair that she didn't mind you pulling on when things started to get good. And even if that sweet young thing did mind…. well, a few tears didn't really put a dent in the whole affair, did it? Matter of fact and truth be told, it kinda made it just that much better, didn't it? After all, only a *real* man could make a woman cry.

A sick little smile crept across his face as he felt the first rush of heat in his loins. He sucked in a lungful of smoke and groped over the curve of his belly to his crotch. Yup, things were starting to come alive down there! It seemed such a shame to keep the good stuff away from his adoring public on a night such as this, but he'd never been one to let an erection go to waste.

"Sorry, girls," he said aloud to all the women of the world, "This one's all mine…."

But just then, he caught sight of something in the corner of his eye. Not much, just the hint of movement off to his right. At first, he ignored it and concentrated on the image of a nameless, faceless woman screaming for him to stop, but then he caught it again. Just the slightest trace of movement; a dark little shadow across a darker background. It wasn't enough to break the mood, but it was just enough to draw his attention, and so he allowed his head to loll idly in that direction even as he stroked his growing erection in his chubby little fist.

At first, he saw nothing; just the square little window and the ugly brown walls, completely bare save for the faded poster of his girl Britney that had occupied its place of honour for too many years to count. He ran his eyes down her bare shoulders and across her flat little belly, and he sneered a grin at the thought of how many times he'd been in this exact same position growing up. A hand full of man-meat, and his eyes on the prize.

Then he saw it. There on the wall, just under Britney's cut-off shorts.

A cockroach.

It was a tiny thing, no bigger across than a fingernail, but its size was hardly the issue. Harold froze for just a second, eyes wide and smoke slowly escaping from his gaping mouth, then he jumped to his knees in the middle of the bed, flaccid cock in one hand and the tail of his cigarette in the other. He remained perfectly still, squatting on his haunches and gaping across at that single cockroach, and all of his childhood fears came back to him in a flood.

Of all the creatures on the planet, the ones he detested most were all of those that crawled or slithered or skittered. And out of that wide array of detestable creatures, the skittering things were the worst. Spiders. Ants. Centipedes. Cockroaches. All of those legs jittering about made his skin crawl. And out of the multitude of skittering things that should die in a fire, the worst of the lot were cockroaches. They were dirty, they were disgusting, they spread filth everywhere they went, and even if you managed to hit the little fuckers hard enough to squash any spider or ant into dust, more often than not a cockroach would just shrug it off and keep skittering away.

Jesus Lord-a'Mighty, how many times had he done battle with those ugly little bastards in this creepy old house over the years? A million? And how many times had he wanted to scream and cry and run upstairs, but didn't because those two old fogeys were the only ones left in the world who didn't call him a scaredy-cat, and he didn't think he could stand it if they did? A million more? At least that many. Probably more. And so he'd taken care of it himself, every single time. And every single time, his skin crawled and his snot ran and his eyes welled up with tears, and afterwards he'd make some excuse to be upstairs, and he'd sit through Matlock and Maalox and abide the old geezers prattling on about old geezer things just so he could try to forget enough to be able to go back down to that creepy little room for the night.

And now, here he was again. Right back where he'd started.

Bigger, older, fatter, but every bit as scared as that frightened little boy from years ago. But all of those battles hadn't been fought in vain. He'd learned a thing or two along the way, and though the killings had never gotten easier, he'd certainly figured out what to do and what *not* to do.

For instance, he knew that the slightest movement would only send that ugly little spawn of Satan into a scurrying frenzy that would have it disappearing back into some tiny little crack or crevasse, and that just wouldn't do. He'd made that mistake before, and he'd learned pretty quickly that the only thing worse than doing battle with one of the things he feared most in the world was knowing that one of them was alive somewhere in his room. It meant days of pussy-footing and eyes darting and jumping out of bed in the middle of the night every time an arm hair moved or an ear tickled. No, no, no, he couldn't go through that again. Not again. And so, just as he'd done a million times before, he squatted in the center of the bed, utterly motionless, and began to formulate a plan.

Of course, every battle was different by necessity. Anyone who'd dealt with the bastards could tell you that. One had to take into consideration factors such as location and size of target, angle of descent and transition, proximity of obstacles, means of approach and so on. But no matter the circumstance, the principle was always the same. Find something big and smash the fucker into pulp.

He used to keep a broom tucked in behind the door for just such an occasion, but it had disappeared in the intervening years. No doubt, his mother had found it and returned it to the hall closet. Well okay then, without his weapon of choice, it was back to the basics. There was a magazine on the floor beside the bed. Not optimum, but it would have to do. Moving with the speed of a sloth then, he stuck his bare ass in the air and reached down for the magazine, then he settled himself back on his rump and slowly began manoeuvring his feet out from underneath his body, always with one eye on that speck on the wall. And a long thirty seconds later, he was sitting on the edge of the bed, big belly resting on his thighs and the latest issue of *Jugs-n-Rugs* rolled it into a tight cylinder.

A shudder rippled up his spine at the thought of going into battle naked, but he had no choice. The fucker wasn't about to stay put while he got dressed, now would it? He choked down his fear and took a single step forward, but with even that little bit of movement, the ugly skittery thing lifted a leg in the air, freezing him to the spot. Several seconds passed, and the leg finally went back down, so he chanced a second step. And then a third. And when he was close enough to see the cockroach in all of its hideous detail, he screwed up the very last of his courage and lunged, swinging the rolled-up magazine as hard as he possibly could.

The Hellspawn must have seen its doom at the very last moment, but by then it was too late. There was a flurry of legs as the thing attempted a mad dash across the wall, but the Jugs-n-Rugs caught it mid-stride, and its plump little body splattered with the sickening *pop!* of an overripe grape.

Harold grimaced in revulsion as he pulled the magazine away and saw the sticky mess left behind, then revulsion turned to horror as the glob of goo peeled away from the wall and plopped to the floor.

He dropped the magazine and jumped back with a startled, "Cocksucker!" but then he caught himself and stood there for a long while to make certain that the ugly little knot of gore was well and truly dead.

And it was, most assuredly. The thing was as dead as could be. Some of its guts were still on the wall, and as hard as the bastards were to kill, he was quite certain that not even a cockroach could survive without its guts. So, okay then. But now came the second part, and it was always nearly as bad as the first. He helped himself to a thick handful of Kleenex from the box on the nightstand, and with a bravery born entirely of necessity, he returned to the site of the execution and wiped the remaining gore from the wall. He threw that handful of tissues into the wastebasket with a shudder, then he helped himself to an even thicker handful and stooped to collect the body itself. He had to struggle for several agonizing moments to fish the mutilated bits of gore from the deep-pile carpet, and more than once he tasted bile at the back of his throat, but then he had it, and he immediately hurried away with the balled-up Kleenex at arm's length directly to the bathroom at the end of the hall.

He was almost there when he thought he could feel something wet soaking through the Kleenex, and he almost dropped it in disgust, but then the last little bit of reason prevailed. No way could such a tiny amount of goo soak through that much padding. It was his imagination playing tricks on him, that's all. But even if the sensation of wetness was false, wasn't there something else?

Couldn't he just feel the rough outline of a hard little kernel between finger and thumb even though he was holding the tissues as loosely as he dared? Kind of like that full, nasty feel the Kleenex takes on after you blow a load of snot into it? Briefly, ever so briefly, he considered pulling the tissues apart to view the remains in the same way that he always checked out whatever he'd ejected from his nose, but it wasn't difficult to deny that particular urge. Just knowing what he held in his hand was enough. If he saw it, he'd puke for sure.

He managed to get the thing all the way to the bathroom and drop it unceremoniously into the toilet, but as he pushed the handle and stood there watching to make certain the ball of Kleenex disappeared for good, every swirl it made around the bowl had the tissues soaking up more and more blue-tinted water, and they quickly began to grow translucent and pull apart, one by one. And like a man happening upon the scene of an accident, Harold just couldn't tear his eyes away from that swirling, spreading sight until a thick, dark lump became visible between the wet folds of Kleenex. He dry-heaved once and only once, then the thing dropped into the whirlpool and shlurped out of sight.

But the job wasn't done yet. He returned to his room, built another pad of Kleenex and gave the wall another scrubbing, then he looked to the floor to make certain he'd gotten every bit of the thing. To his disgust, he discovered a single hairlike limb hanging onto a few carpet fibres for dear life, but he managed to snare it with a second pass and was soon flushing again. At last, he collected the despoiled magazine and thew it in the wastebasket, then he carried the basket upstairs, opened the front door, and flung the whole thing out into the yard as far as he could.

That last bit of business seen to, he retired back down to his room and lit a smoke, then he perched himself on the edge of the bed and let out a long, shaky sigh. He took a few moments to calm his nerves and purge the gruesome images from his mind, and in a cumulative attack of the willies, he gave a violent shudder and emitted a horrified, "Fuck!" to the empty room.

It was time he put on some clothes. If he had his way, he'd stay naked as a jaybird all night long, doing whatever came naturally, but he suddenly felt very…. exposed. It was five minutes too late, he knew, but covering his nakedness even at this late stage would at least help beat back the willies. After all, he told himself, no one ever saw a soldier go into battle in his altogether, right? Hell, maybe that was even why uniforms had been invented in the first place. So that Generals didn't have to go to war with their Privates hanging out.

Allowing himself a self-satisfied smirk at his own cleverness, he reached down for his jeans laying in a pile on the floor and pulled them up to his lap. He never wore underwear, rather preferring the feel of his little buddy hanging loose, so he slipped one chubby leg into the pants, and then the other, and then he stood to make carefully certain that everything was in its proper position before reaching under his belly to pull up the zipper.

And that's when he saw it. Right there. Right there on his leg. A hideous black cockroach the size of a child's fist. Right there on his goddam *leg!*

Neither of them moved. Not at first. After hiding out in the folds of his jeans and hitching a ride up, the creature simply clung there against his thigh, staring up at the human suddenly frozen in fear. Harold heard a strangely familiar sucking of air and realized it was he, then he let out a childlike mewl and felt his throat tighten around the sound until he was no longer breathing at all.

And it was at that precise moment that the cockroach moved.

It twitched its antennae and lifted a single accusing limb into the air, aiming it directly up at the man, but even then, Harold was frozen to the spot. This was every childhood fear quite literally coming home to roost, and he couldn't move a single solitary muscle. This was no fingernail-sized cockroach clinging to a wall. This was the grand-daddy of all bugs, and it was *on* him! It was fucking *on* him!

At last, he drew back a hand as if he might've actually intended to sweep the thing away as easily as he would a bit of lint, but that was as far as it went. He simply couldn't bring himself to do it. As horrifying as it was to have that awful creature on his body, actually *touching* the thing was too dreadful to even contemplate. Plus, there was the added bonus that even if he somehow managed the impossible, he would be knocking the thing straight down toward his bare feet. But even as he stood there, frozen in fear, he knew that the stalemate would never last. If he didn't do something and do it soon, that son of a bitch would eventually move, and when it did, it would sure as shit move in the direction it was already pointed.

Straight.

Fucking.

Up.

In his mind, he saw the thing skitter the rest of the way up his pant leg and then across his naked belly, tangling and untangling itself through his mat of hair. And before he could stop it, it would scurry up to his face, using one finger-sized forelimb to probe the tender meat at the corner of his lips. And when he let loose with the scream that was sure to follow, the thing would crawl right into his open, gaping mouth.

With that final horrifying vision, and with a courage manifest not just of desperation now but of abject panic, he did the unthinkable. He actually swatted at the giant cockroach with his bare hand. There was a momentary sensation of something wet and pulpy against his skin, and then something hard, and then everything after that became a blur. Thankfully, his first strike connected, for he knew with absolute certainty that he'd never be able to manage a second no matter the circumstances, and the creature sailed several feet through the air in an arc, wriggling its hundreds of ugly little legs all the way. But the bastard somehow managed to right itself mid-flight and land far too softly on the thick carpeting, and it immediately spun around, turned its horrible buggy eyes directly on him, and reared up like a cobra.

And then it attacked. Unbelievably, the thing charged straight at him, and with no time to think, Harold flung himself backwards onto the bed, shaking the bed frame down to its core and slamming the headboard hard against the wall. He flipped himself around quickly enough to make his man-breasts swing like twin pendulums and ended in a crouch on his hands and knees, but when he looked to the floor where he'd last seen the creature, it was no longer there.

For one awful moment, the frightened boy-Harold thought he could no longer see it because surely the thing was climbing up the side of the bed even now. But then the adult-Harold balled up his courage enough to finally crawl close enough to peer over the edge, and he saw nothing. No giant skittery thing climbing up the bed linen. Nothing lying in wait. He squinted against the growing darkness and scanned every inch of the floor from one corner to the other and back again, but there was nothing there. Nothing at all.

But of course not. That's not how those creepy-ass bastards

worked, was it? No, of course not. The little ones were stupid, coming out in the open and alighting on walls and such. But the big ones got big because they were smarter. They hid. And where would a monster as big as a child's fist hide itself? Where else but with all the other monsters.

It was under the bed, sure as shit. He knew it as sure as he knew his own name. It was under there, and just as with every other monster that lived under every bed, the rules were clear. It would stay under their, lurking and waiting, and as soon as a foot touched the ground, it would attack. He would feel it first as a gentle tickle on his bare toes, then he'd feel a million skittery little legs across the top of his foot. Then those horrible skittery legs would start crawling up his leg, but the bastard will have learned a lesson from its last attack. This time, it would skitter up *inside* his pants where he couldn't brush it away. He'd feel it crawl up his shin, and over his knee. Then he'd feel it on his bare thigh. And then he'd feel it on his crotch, but it wouldn't be able to go any farther. The tight waistband of his jeans would trap it there, so maybe it would just crawl up under his ball sack and make a nest. And then it would get hungry and.....

Jesus! He did his best to purge the horrible images from his mind, but it did little to allay his fear. Just as it had been twenty-odd years ago when he knew with absolute certainty that the Bogey Man himself resided under this very bed in this very room, he was suddenly afraid to step off his own bed. It was ridiculous, he knew, but he also knew that he wasn't wrong. He looked to the door, eight feet away, and remembered how he used to try making that giant leap in a single bound to keep out of the monster's grasp. It had been an impossible feat back then, but he was bigger now. He was taller. His legs were longer. Surly he could jump eight feet now, right? Hell, *anyone* could jump eight feet, for *crissakes!* But even if he managed the jump, there was a ninety degree turn to get through the doorway, and no one could turn in midair.

No one but a cockroach.....

No matter, though. So, he'd land just inside the door. So what? The door was open. All he had to do was step through. Hell, he'd *run* through it if he felt like it. In fact, maybe he'd skip on through and prance down the hallway singing 'I'm a little fucking teapot' if the mood struck him. Shit, he'd prance and skip and scream like a goddam *girl* if he felt like it! Who'd see him? Who'd laugh? And anyway, would running out of his room at the thought of a Bogey-Cockroach make him any less of a man than crouching ass-high atop a spongey mattress as his little-boy testicles rose up into his abdomen?

"Fuck no," he told himself out loud, "And fuck you, too!" he added in a downward direction, liking the way it sounded just a bit like Schwarzenegger in one of his blow-the-world-to-Hell movies.

And so, just as his courage was coiled up as tight as it was ever going to get, he eased into a crouch and crept to the edge of the mattress closest to the door, then he took a moment to actually picture himself flying through the air like a gymnast. He'd stick the landing on one foot, spin, and bound effortlessly through the door. No problem. Piece of goddam cake. He hauled himself up to a squat and had one more quick look to make sure the coast was clear, then he hooked his toes over the bed frame, and with only the briefest of hesitations, hurled himself through the air.

He landed well short, and he hit hard. His big belly bounced, his man-breasts jiggled, and a sharp pain shot straight through his knee. But he'd hit the ground in a semblance of a run, so he made the ninety-degree turn somewhat less clumsily than a water buffalo and blundered his way through the open doorway..... and then he stopped. It was only the briefest of pauses to look back with a triumphant sneer and perhaps salvage what he could of his manhood, but it was the wrong move. The big black monster skittered out from under the bed like a multi-limbed hound from Hell and ran straight at him.

Once again, he was frozen with fear. The little boy had known what would happen, but the adult had apparently still been clinging to it's grand illusions by the ragged ends of its fingertips. It was a *cockroach*, for crissakes! A fucking *insect!* He must have outweighed the thing by a gazillion to one! And yet the boy had known. He had known it all along. And now, here was the grown-up version of that child, cowering and quivering and scared to goddam death because of a mother-fucking bug!

It skitter-charged directly toward the open doorway, and in that brief eternity of seconds, the reasoning adult became the little boy again. He uttered a frightened, girlish squeal and ran down the hallway to the stairs, then he took the stairs two at a time and didn't stop until he was safely at the top. Then and only then, heart pounding and breath coming in rapid pants, he finally turned and looked down the stairs. He half-expecting to see the horrible thing skittering up after him, hissing like a feral beast, but he saw nothing.

The monster was gone.

He stood there for a moment longer, bent at the waist and wheezing like an asthmatic, and once adult-Harold was back in charge, he huffed his contempt down the stairs, turned, and stormed across the entranceway into the kitchen. There, he started throwing cupboard doors open at random, slamming some immediately shut with a snort and pawing through others with the desperation of a junkie looking for a fix. What he was looking for was there somewhere. He knew it was. He'd seen it more than once. The Hellspawn cockroaches might have stayed well clear of the main floor, but the old lady was a fanatic when it came to flying insects breaking the sanctity of her kitchen. It was hilarious considering her complete inability to so much as boil water, but maybe she was afraid that even a fly would turn up its nose at her cooking. Either way, he knew it was there. Somewhere.

And sure enough, there it was, under the sink and half-hidden by a box of dishwasher detergent. The label showed a cartoon housefly on its back, with its legs in the air and little x's for eyes. The name on the can was 'Attack', and it promised to make any bug 'Dead, dead, *dead* in seconds flat!' He would have been more confident if the cartoon bug had been an ugly-ass cockroach lying tits-up, but what the hell. If it killed a fly as dead as Elvis, it would work on anything that skittered. And like the label said, 'the only good bug is a dead bug'.

He gave the trigger a test squeeze and sneered a grin. The sound made by a can of insecticide was like nothing else on the planet, and the acrid stench had a smell all its own. It sounded like business, and it stunk like death.

*I love the smell of bug killer in the morning.....*he thought crazily, heading back down the stairs one slow step at a time. *Yessiree, gonna make me a whole messa killin'.....*

He reached the bottom step feeling confident enough to take on the world, but then he took the final step and felt the deep nap of the carpet between his bare toes, and a nervous twitch shivered up his spine. For a moment, he considered going back up for the shoes he'd so casually kicked into the hall closet, but he was honest enough with himself to know that if he were to go back upstairs, the chances of him having the balls to come back down were something close to zero. So he'd be stuck up there, consigned to sleeping on the livingroom sofa, and there he would stay for the rest of his life with his parents clucking their disapproval every time he was within earshot. And he'd have to take every bit of it, because they'd be right. He'd have proven himself to be the big baby everyone always said he was.

No, no, no. Shoes or no shoes, he had to do this, and he had to do it quickly, before he had time to reconsider.

"Come on you little prick….." he said aloud without much conviction, stepping cautiously toward the bedroom while scanning the floor for any sign of movement, "Come and get your poison….."

Before he'd gotten halfway there, something scurried through his peripheral vision and he immediately wheeled right, blasting out a fog of spray. But it struck nothing. He must have imagined that flicker of movement. But had he? The hallway was long and narrow, so a bug would've had to have been a ninja to get away so fast, but those little bastards moved so fast! It was possible, wasn't it? There *could* have been a bug there, couldn't it? Here one second and gone the next? Hell, that was the calling card of *all* little skittering things, wasn't it?

For a moment, he was torn between hunting for the hallway ninja or continuing on with his original mission, but there was no real choice. The priority had to be in ridding his room of the big mother fucker, and once that was done, he could take his sweet-ass time probing all of the dark corners of the basement to make sure there were no more.

A few more steps brought him to the open doorway of the bedroom, and he stopped once again. Some little part of him had expected the monster to be waiting just beyond the threshold, but of course it had just been that little-boy fear talking. The thing was nowhere to be seen. Still, he craned his neck and peered in as far as he could without setting a single foot inside the room, and when he saw no sign of the monster, he finally breathed a sigh of relief. Obviously, it had gone about its ugly little bug business after he'd
    fled?…..
left the room. And even more obviously, those people who said

things like, 'it's more frightened of you than you are of it' were spot-on correct. Yes, in the cold light of reason, he knew deep down that those people were undoubtedly right. Even deeper down though, down in the place where things went bump in the night and not every dark, hulking shape was merely a shadow, he wondered if people only said those things because the truth was simply too awful to imagine.

Another chill shivered up his spine, and he immediately chided himself. It was a *bug*, for crissakes! A stupid, brainless bug! Ugly as hell and creepy as fuck, sure, but it was just a *bug!* No doubt, the bastard had scurried back under the bed or scooted around behind the dresser and was even now cowering in fear. Fear at the return of the massive human who shit things bigger than it on any given day. Fear at the giant that could stomp it into the ground if he was of a mind. Fear at the gigantic human with his aerosol can of death!

He felt a sneer creep back across his thin, bloodless lips, and he stepped into the room. And before his newfound courage had time to wain, he went right up to the bed, dropped to his knees, stuck his ass high in the air, and peered underneath.

At first, he could see nothing. Then, as his eyes began to adjust to the darkness, dim shapes began to coalesce out of the gloom. There was something large and square at the far end. A box. An apple box that he had stashed there himself that very morning, filled with a few of his more peculiar…..eccentricities. And behind and around the box were dust bunnies; aptly named, apparently, because they were everywhere! Idly, he wondered when the underside of this bed had last seen the business end of a vacuum cleaner, and just as idly, he decided that it may never have done. But then he started to make something else out, huddled up amidst the dust bunnies. Something darker, more angular. Probably something he'd drop-kicked under there as a child, no doubt. A ball, maybe? Or a toy? He squinted against the darkness and tried to make out that single dark shape, and he quickly came to the conclusion that it was too oddly-shaped to be a ball. So one of his action figures, then. Hey, maybe it was even his long-lost Stretch Armstrong!

All at once, the prospect of reclaiming a lost treasure from his youth pushed aside all other thoughts, and he scooted around the side of the bed and reached under to claim his prize. But just as he was about to close his hand around the thing, his eyes finally adjusted to the darkness enough for him to see the thing for what it really was.

There, squatting motionless among the dust bunnies like a beast hiding in the tall grass, was the silhouette of a massive cockroach the size of a child's fist.

He recoiled in horror and emitted an audible squeal, but at least he had the presence of mind to remember the mission. He brought up the can of Attack, aimed it directly at the filthy creature, and fired.

Now, the monster moved. As the first droplets touched its skin, it skittered to one side, but then the fog filled the entire underside of the bed, and it reversed direction. And then it set about a frenzied dance, skittering through the dust bunnies in one direction and then the other, twirling and spinning in its desperation to escape. But wherever it went, the spray followed, and at last, its crazy dance slowed and it staggered back to the wall as the poisonous mist coated its entire body with a filmy white froth.

"*Die*, goddamit!" Harold swore at the creature, "Just fucking *die* already!"

The stench of chemicals filled his nostrils and stung his eyes, and he finally released the trigger. And as the heavy mist settled to the floor, he could finally make out the hideous creature huddled up against the baseboard, coated in a thick layer of bubbling foam. He could detect no movement from the thing, but just in case it was a trick, he gave the creature one more quick blast, and when it rolled onto its back and curled its hideous legs over its fat, bloated body, he knew for certain that it was dead.

"*Gotcha*, you sunovabitch!" he declared aloud to the room, then in a series of butt-high manoeuvres that had his all-too-feminine breasts penduluming every which way but complimentarily, he took to scanning every inch of the underside of the bed to make sure that there were no other bastards hiding in the shadows. He even gave a few test-blasts of Attack to see if something sprang out, but the only movement came from dust bunnies being blown back like tumbleweeds in the wind.

Alright then. Good. The monster was dead, and it was high time to implement the next phase of the plan. It wasn't enough that he'd killed the monster. If he every intended to spend another night in this squalid little room, he had to know not only that there were no others hiding under the bed, but that there were no others hiding *anywhere*. Holding the spray can at the ready then, he moved to the rickety TV stand and pulled it away from the wall. It was so precariously balanced that it threatened to topple, but he caught it at the last second and had a peek behind. There were no surprises there, so he left it where it was and peered closely around the base of the headboard for any sign of movement. Again, nothing.

The only other furniture in the room was the dresser near the window, but the thing would be a bitch to move. It was deep and wide, and held twelves drawers stuffed with a boy's lifetime of accumulated crap. He gave the thing a one-handed test pull, but just as he'd figured, the big dresser didn't budge. He tucked the bug spray under an armpit and grabbed one side of the dresser with both hands, and though his face reddened and he grunted with the strain, he at last got the monstrosity to move an inch. Encouraged now, he set the spray can on top of the dresser and put all of his strength into one heavy pull. The thing moved another few inches away from the wall, but the movement was accompanied by a most curious and disconcerting sound, not unlike the tearing of velcro. And almost at once, a bulbous green cockroach the size of a bottle cap lifted itself awkwardly over the back of the dresser and began skittering aimlessly about as if in drunken confusion.

Again came the squeal and the fumbling for the bug spray, and just like the other creature, the fat little bug made a run for it as soon as the trigger was pulled. But by then, it was too late. One prolonged spray later, it crumpled into a foam-covered ball, rolled to the very edge of the dresser, tottered there for one agonizing second, and dropped over the side.

Harold grunted in disgust at having yet another corpse to deal with, but before he could even begin to contemplate how much Kleenex it would take, he caught movement out of the corner of his eye and turned just in time to see a second cockroach appear over the back of the dresser. This one was bigger that the first and moved with lightning speed, but the spray followed it as it tried to make its escape, and it finally curled up into an ugly little ball mere inches from freedom.

But even as that creature died, another appeared over the back of the dresser.

And then another. And another. And another still. And as the steady stream of Attack targeted each one in turn, more came, and then more. At first they came one at a time, then in little bunches of twos and threes, then the wave turned into a torrent and the horrid things all but poured out of the gap. There were huge black things with long bristly legs, smaller creatures that crawled all over one another in their frenzy, and little dime-sized bugs so lightly-coloured as to almost be translucent, and it was all the man could do to wave the spray from side to side and hope that the general all-encompassing mist would be enough to kill them all. He felt bile gurgling at the back of his throat and choked it down, but then his overactive imagination kicked in and he began to feel a thousand tiny little legs crawling all over his body. He felt them skittering across his feet and crawling up his legs, and then he felt them scrambling up his arms and across his face and tangling their thick, gangly legs in his hair, and it took every ounce of intestinal fortitude he could muster to stand firm. Every fibre of his being fairly *screamed* at him to run from the room, but he didn't. Wholly against his nature, he stayed put and kept up the onslaught.

One after another of the horrible creatures succumbed to the spray and crumpled into a foamy white tangle of limbs, and by the time the trigger was released a full three minutes later, not a single cockroach remained alive. Whatever science had gone into creating the deadly spray had proven to be astonishingly effective, and as the fog slowly cleared, Harold stood dumbfounded at the carnage he had wrought.

He didn't do anything as egregious as count the bodies, but he didn't have to. There were dozens. Dozens upon dozens upon dozens. The sight of so many crumpled bodies trapped in the amber of insecticide and scattered all about the floor was almost too much to take, but though the acrid tang of vomit lingered at the back of his throat and his heart pounded a furious drumbeat his ears, his revulsion soon began to give way to something else. It was such an alien feeling that it took him a while to even comprehend what it was, but at last there was no denying it. What he was feeling was pride. Actual, genuine pride! And why not? After all, he could have run. Hell, all things considered, he *should* have run. But he hadn't. He'd stood his ground, and for perhaps the first time in his life, he had proven his mettle.

But even as he stood there savouring his victory, his mind began replaying individual scenes of the event, and his skin crawled anew with the memory of a thousand imagined things skittering all over his body. He closed his eyes and concentrated on dispelling the awful images from his mind, and it seemed to work, for the most part. The ghost bugs eventually vanished and the gooseflesh ultimately abated, and yet one lingering sensation remained. He could still feel a gentle and most disturbing tickling against the side of one bare foot.

Well, no wonder. The carpet was deep, and his feet were bare. It was a stray carpet fibre, no more. He ignored the tickling for a second or two, and when it persisted, his other foot came over to satisfy the itch. It was a reflexive thing, an act so natural and commonplace that a person might perform it a hundred times a day and not even be aware. A nerve ending is stimulated, the subconscious mind registers it as a tickle or an itch, and the body responds without thought. But in this case, instead of a big toe simply sweeping the tickle away, it came upon something unfamiliar, and then the toe *itself* began to tickle. And with that disturbance in an otherwise autonomic act, the subconscious mind alerted the conscious, and Harold at last turned a casual eye downward.

For one fleeting moment, he thought that his foot must have grown an extra toe. And a black one, at that. But no, it wasn't a sixth toe. It was a big black cockroach, curled up against his foot as if it were the only place in the room left to hide.

The man shrieked and leaped into the air, and the sudden movement sent the cockroach into a veritable frenzy. It skittered first one way and then the other, and with the idea of stomping on the creature in his bare feet simply too unimaginable to contemplate, Harold was resigned to hopping from foot to foot and dancing about like a crazy man to keep out of its way. At last, the creature made a mad dash for the underside of the dresser, and it was all Harold could do to send a poorly-aimed stream of Attack after it, accompanied by a string of his most expressive curses.

And then, whether it was a lingering sense of pride or a pure unabiding rage that drove him on, he again tucked the insecticide under his arm, grabbed a double handful of dresser, and wrenched the ungainly thing a full foot away from the wall, But just as he reacquired the trigger and was about to lean around for a clear shot at the escapee, something long and slender emerged out of this newly-made gap, freezing him to the spot. At first, he had the insane notion that a rat was somehow backing itself up the backside of the dresser, tail-first, but then a second slender twitching thing appeared, followed immediately by a huge pair of compound eyes and the leading edge of a carapace as wide across as a soup bowl. Then the rest of a monstrous cockroach squeezed itself up through the gap and plopped its bulk exhaustedly down on the top of the dresser.

Harold was at once horrified and fascinated by the sheer size of the creature, and though he initially shied back a few staggered steps, he couldn't tear his eyes away from the thing. Until that very moment, he had only seen cockroaches as little round skittery things or ugly flattened lumps of indefinable goo, but the creature squatting there knee-deep in foam was so huge that he could at last see his mortal enemy in all of its grotesque glory.

The shell was elongated, tapering toward a rounded point at the rear, and though it glistened like wet leather, it appeared to be as thick and formidable as that of any tortoise. Six long, multi-jointed legs splayed out in the foam, each one as long as man's finger and covered from end to end with sharp pointed protrusions like the thorns of a rosebush. But as hideous as the body was, it was the head that captivated Harold's attention. The thing was tear-shaped and appeared at first strangely small for the body size, but Harold quickly realized that he was seeing only a portion of it. The leading edge of the sturdy carapace covered much of it, and most of the lower half was buried in foam.

This last actually gave Harold some bit of comfort, even considering the immense size of the thing. With its face and mouth buried in insecticide, the creature must surely die, and quickly. In fact, it might be dead even now, for all he knew. But no sooner had the idea occurred to him than the creature heaved its big tear-shaped head out of the foam and wagged a bristly forelimb in the air, then it launched itself across the dresser, directly at him.

Harold was quick on the trigger, but the fresh blast of poison barely slowed the creature. It charged across the dresser in the face of the storm, then the can sputtered its last and there was only one thing Harold could do. In a fit of madness, he raised the empty can of Attack high above his head, and slammed it down as hard as he could in the exact center of the creature's body.

The carapace cracked open with the sound of splintered bone, and a black viscous goo squirted out like toothpaste from a tube. But though the creature was mortally wounded, it wasn't yet done. It hauled itself along on its forelimbs, dragging a trail of gore inch by disgusting inch, but then the can came down again and tore the massive body completely in two, and at last the creature slumped lifelessly into the foam.

Harold dropped the empty can to the floor, released a breath that he might be holding onto for years as he tried to quell a sickening churning, deep in his belly. But then he took a step back and felt something wet and pulpy pop beneath his heel, and he had to choke back a throatful of vomit as he dragged his foot across the carpet and saw the blue streak of gore left behind. But though the battle had hardly ended on a high note, at least it was done. The nightmare was over, at last.

Picking his way carefully now, like a soldier tiptoeing through a minefield, he got himself to where he could peer behind the dresser, and sure enough, he could plainly see a huge gap of some five or six inches running along the baseboards. But this was no artifact of shoddy construction. The edges were rough and uneven, and the carpet was stained by a dust as fine as talc, ground into it by a million tiny feet.

So this was the nest, then. What might once have been a hairline crack in the plaster had given the first few bastards a place of refuge, but those initial few had enlarged the nest. And as their size and numbers grew, so did the opening. Now, it was big enough to allow a cockroach the size of the bisected monstrosity lying dead atop the dresser to squeeze through.

As hard as it was for Harold to imagine so much activity going on right under his nose, an even more horrible thought suddenly occurred to him. How would so many cockroaches possibly feed themselves? Scraps of food and dropped breadcrumbs? Well, he'd certainly left his share of dirty dishes lying around as a kid, but would that have been enough? It didn't seem plausible. Other bugs, then? Probably. He'd sure never seen a spider or an ant in the house, but it still didn't seem like it would be enough.

And that's when he realized the truth. An army that size would have to scour every corner of this room and beyond every night in order to find enough food. Every one of those thousands of nights he'd slept in his bed, the nest had emptied, flooding the room. They'd skittered up the walls, and in and out of dresser drawers, and across the ceiling. Hell, they must have skittered over every square inch of this dark little room.....

Christ!

Every square inch. Every square inch, including the bed. How many times over all of those years had he awoken in the middle of the night to a vague discomfort and a curious itch. How often had he slept while they'd scurried through the bedsheets? Had they come every night, crawling over every inch of his sleeping body?

Though the very idea shook him to the core, it also filled him with resolve.

"Fuck that!" he cursed, pounding out of the bedroom and taking the stairs two at a time.

He'd never used the thing, but he knew where to find it. And sure enough, there it was, tucked into the corner of the little closet next to the upstairs bathroom. It was the sturdy, barrel-shaped body of the ElectroShag vacuum cleaner he'd heard roaring over his head every Sunday morning when everyone in their right mind was trying to get a few more hours of sleep. Though he'd always abhorred the idea of performing anything even approaching housekeeping, desperate times called for desperate measures, so he rolled the thing out on its tiny little wheels with its power cord rolled up behind its ass like a curly tail and its long hose retracted into its face like a big fat snout.

He thumped the squat little pig down the stairs and quickly found an outlet to plug the thing in, then he toggled the switch and the beast roared to life with a belch of exhaust that smelled mildly of old farts. A devilish grin crossed his thin, angry lips as he dragged the little pig to the threshold of his bedroom, and he stood there for a long moment to savour the site of his ultimate victory and the lingering stench of insecticide.

At last, he stepped into the room and set to work.

The first order of business was to make sure that there were no more surprises hiding in the carpet, so he cleared a safe path right up to the bed, then he dropped to his knees and shoved the working end of the ElectroShag as far under as he could reach. He swept it back and forth and felt the thing jump in his hand with every hard little nugget that bounced through the hose, and when the jumping stopped, he crouched as low as he could get and worked the nozzle with rather more precision. The big, foam-caked body of his original victim was still there, pasted up against the headboard, but aside from a host of dust bunnies beyond the reach of the initial sweep of the nozzle, it was alone. He aimed the nozzle at the corpse, and as he approach it inch by careful inch, the thing began to stir and tremble as if it were cowering in fear, but then suction finally overcame adhesion and the horrible thing bumped its way up the hose with a wet *thunk! thunk! thunk!*

A few more sweeps of the nozzle was enough to clear out the last of the dust bunnies, and a close inspection of every dark corner revealed no more surprises, so Harold stood, tugged the seam of his jeans out of his butt crack, and turned to the site of the real carnage.

Jesus, this next bit was going to tax his nerves to the limit! Yes, the bugs were all dead, but there were so damn many of them! He purposely averted his eyes from the horror atop the dresser and concentrated instead on the somewhat easier job of cleaning up the dozens that that lay scattered in ugly little knots on the floor, half-hidden in the deep pile of the carpet. They thunked and thwatted and splatted all the way up the hose, each one sending a corresponding shiver up Harold's spine, but the ElectroShag was a hardy little pig. Even the purple streak of gore he'd pawed from the sole of his foot vanished without a trace. Only once did he have a nervous moment, and that was when one of the loathsome lumps of supposedly lifeless meat stirred into a hellish bandy-legged thing as the nozzle drew near and retreated in a desperate skitter, back toward the nest. The thing had either been barely clinging to life or had taken to hiding among the corpses, but either way, the ElectroShag caught the reanimated bastard before it had traveled a yard, and it disappeared into the nozzle. The hose jumped and bumped as if the creature were fighting for a foothold all the way, but it didn't last long. And with the little pig purring along nicely and the floor entirely rid of land mines, Harold finally turned his attention to the grotesquery on top of the dresser.

Dozens upon dozens of tangled little bodies lay pasted to the surface by the foam, and he had some concern whether or not the vacuum cleaner was up to task. But ultimately, he needn't have worried. A quick pass along the nearest edge removed corpses and foam alike, and the little pig took it all in stride. So Harold pressed on. He swept the nozzle across the battlefield like a broom, wincing in disgust as every corpse thumped its way up the hose, but never stopping. And before long, most of the job was done. All that remained was the the big monster he'd purposely left to the end, and in this, his concerns about the pig's power proved entirely valid. The bisected creature maintained a death grip on the dresser until the last of the foam was gone, then it gave a final shudder and finally succumbed to the powerful suction. But that was as far as it went. Even cut in two, the thing was simply too big for the hose to swallow, and its back-half ended up stuck in the mouth of the nozzle, causing the roar of the little pig to wind itself up into a high-pitched squeal. But just as Harold began to worry that he'd have to take a more....*hands-on* approach to the dilemma, the blockage folded in on itself and squeezed through the nozzle with a wet, sickening *shhlooop!* The ElectroShag whined once more as the corpse became stuck halfway up the hose, but then the nozzle jumped like a bucking bronco, the whine turned back to a roar, and Harold turned to the infinitely more loathsome front half of the creature. It's antennae waggled and its forelimbs danced a little jig as the vacuum approached, but then the pig gave a mighty squeal and the horrid thing *shlooped* up and out of sight.

With that last of the corpses gone, Harold tucked the hose under an armpit, took hold of the dresser in both hands, and pulled it far away from the wall. And after cleaning up the few bodies that had fallen down that way, he turned the little pig loose on the nest itself. He shoved the nozzle as far as he could into the crack in the wall, and when he felt it jump in his hands, he began sweeping it from side to side and alternatively withdrawing it a few inches and stabbing it deeper and deeper into the nest. The hose jumping more than a dozen times, but at last it lay still for a full minute or more no matter which way the nozzle was pointed, so he withdrew it at last, certain that the nest was now well and truly emptied.

Now, there was only one more thing he had to do. There was a closet on the far side of the bed, and he hadn't so much as cracked either of its bi-fold doors in the better part of ten years. If any of the bastards still lived, sure as shit, that was where they would be.

He circled the bed, lugging the ElectroShag behind, and poised himself before the closed doors. He took a deep breath to steady his nerves, and when he thought that he was as ready as he would ever be, he flung open first one door and then the other, and dropped the nozzle to the floor.

Thankfully though, the mad charge he'd half-expected didn't

happen. All within seemed as it always had. Clothes hanging. Board games piled in a corner. Shoes and toys and the oddments of an abandoned childhood scattered all over the floor. There were dust bunnies here, too, but the ElectroShag made quick work of them until one of them sprang suddenly to life and made a break for it. Harold was forced to take a frightened step backward, but one quick thrust of the nozzle later, and the moment's drama was over as quickly as it had begun.

He sneered and gave a hard enough kick to the stack of board games to send them all tumbling to the floor, and sure enough, in amongst the jumble of houses and hotels and paper money was a single brown cockroach the approximate size of a well-fed rat. It shied away, backing up against the wall, then it proceeded to skitter back and forth in a frantic search for a hiding spot. But with no place nearly large enough to accommodate its bulk, it suddenly turned and launched itself directly toward the open doors.

Again, Harold back-pedalled and brought to ElectroShag to bear, but he was too slow and the creature was too fast. With nowhere else to go, he was forced to leap bodily onto the bed and watch the creature disappear underneath, but he knew that it would never stay there. With all of its hiding places gone and the stench of insecticide hanging thick in the air, the thing would make for the nest, sure as hell. He tugged at the hose to give himself as much slack as he could and spun around to face the other side of the bed, and when the creature dutifully reappeared in a flurry of legs, he brought the nozzle down on top of it like the tip of a lance. He stabbed right through the thing and pinned it to the spot, but it was simply too big for the ElectroShag's to swallow. The creature wriggled about, pawing at the carpet in its desperation to escape, but Harold was undaunted. He put all of his weight into one final thrust, driving the nozzle bodily through the creature, and the wriggling finally ceased. Then the little pig set to work, and Harold was witness to a curious and most unsettling display. Unable to take the whole thing at once, the vacuum cleaner first emptied the creature's body of all of its contents as if sucking a milkshake up a straw, then the hollowed-out body collapsed in on itself like a balloon deflating, and at last it shlucked into the nozzle, bumping its way along the entire length of the hose.

More determined now than ever, Harold returned to the closet and began kicking aside boxes and smacking at the hanging clothes and sucking up anything and everything the vacuum could manage. Game pieces, scattered hockey cards, the odd sock; whatever was in the way was resigned to the belly of the pig. He shoved the nozzle between boxes and boardgames and discarded shoes, and he used it to swat at shirts and sweaters and his old jeans jacket hanging from the rod, then he worked it into every corner and along every edge of every wall and as high up toward the ceiling as he could reach. But with all of that labour, there was really only one more encounter. He had just manoeuvred the business end of the ElectroShag behind a particularly dusty box in the back corner when the machine's motor whined and the hose contracted as something thick and heavy blocked the flow of air. But he stabbed frantically into the corner a few times, dislodged and broke apart whatever had caused the obstruction, and something not unlike several pieces of wet sponge passed up the hose.

And with that, he was done. With this last possible bug sanctuary seen to, he was absolutely certain that he'd gotten every last one of the bastards. He was spent, physically and emotionally, his back was drenched with sweat, his hair stuck up in crazy spikes and swirls, and his backed ached something fierce. But it was finally over. He'd done it. He'd actually done it. He'd faced his fears, and he'd vanquished his foe.

He ran a hand through his hair and plucked at the uncomfortable feel of the moist waistband tucked under his protruding belly, then he planted his fists into the small of his back and stretched until he could hear his spine creak and feel little pops all along his backbone. And as he dragged the ElectroShag out into the hallway and became aware of a dull throbbing at the back of his head, he spared a moment to ponder just how much damage he might've done to himself at breathing in so much insecticide. But no matter. It wasn't so much that it couldn't be fixed by a cold beer or ten, after all. And he was assured of a peaceful night to sleep it all off, so *huzzah* to the victor over the skittery things!

He reached for the switch to shut down the vacuum, but then another thought occurred to him, and he left it running as he returned to the closet and grabbed a shirt at random from the hangers. He then went back to the ElectroShag and stuffed the shirt as far up the little pig's snout as he could to form a tight plug, and only then did he toggle it off. Just in case anything was still alive in there, that would keep them in the belly of the pig. Later, he'd take the whole thing outside and hurl it out into the front yard. Or maybe he'd pour some lighter fluid over the thing and have himself a bonfire. Hell, maybe he'd just throw the whole damn thing over the fence and let old Jimmy Stanton deal with whatever might happen to crawl out.

But whatever. He'd figure that part out later. For now, all he wanted was to rest and to bathe in his triumph.

He returned to the bedroom -- *his* bedroom and his *alone*, he concluded smugly -- and plopped himself down on the foot of the bed. He retrieved his pack of smokes from the ugly little table, fingered one out, lit it, and inhaled a double lungful of heavenly smoke to wash away the acrid aftertaste of the insecticide. He leaned his head back on aching shoulders and blew a column of smoke at the ceiling, but now he found himself regarding that ceiling with a new fascination. How many times had he looked up at that celing as a child and seen something scampering over his head? Now, he never would again. He allowed his eyes to play over the ceiling and down to the wall behind the dresser, and he gave himself a smirk. He could gaze at that wall for the rest of eternity and he'd never see another cockroach.

Goddamn he was happy with himself!

"Fuck you all," he said out loud, but his throat was raw and his mouth was dry, so the words came out less confidently than he would have liked. Still, the rasp made him sound kind of bad-ass, so he laid back on the bed and drew smoke deep down into his lungs through lips curled into a mean little grin.

He smoked the cigarette down to the nub and stubbed out the last bit of it into an overflowing ashtray as he crawled to his feet. His head still ached like a sunovabitch, and now there was a knot in his back, too. What he needed was a handful of Tylenol and a few tall, cold beers to wash them all down. Hell, maybe he'd even help himself to the old man's Chivas and let the old geezer bitch. With all he'd been through, he'd damn-well earned himself a good drunk.

He stood there for a moment, rolling his head from side to side and listening to his neck crack and pop in a dozen different places, then he passed back out into the hallway and bent to gather up the ElectroShag.....

And that's when he saw it.

There, standing stock-still in the very center of the hallway, was a big, black cockroach as wide across as a dinner plate.

The sight of the thing froze Harold in place. His breath hitched in his throat, his jaw grew slack, and he found himself utterly unable to move a single muscle. He remained rooted to the spot even as the massive creature reared back, lifted a forelimb into the air, and pointed it accusingly at Sam.

Then, it hissed. It actually *hissed!*

The horror of the moment was not lost on Harold. A bubble of methane erupted from between his clenched buttocks and a narrow crescent of wetness spread across his crotch, but at last he was able to move, if only to take a single, faltering step backward. Then he took another step, and then another and another, not once taking his eyes from the massive creature. He groped his way back, farther and farther, until he finally reached his bedroom door. But just as he was about to disappear back into his room, the creature made its move.

It launched itself down the hallway with an almost audible pounding of legs on the floor, and even as Harold leaped back and swung his bedroom door closed, there came a heavy *thud!* from the opposite side that shook the door in its frame, followed immediately by something like teeth clicking, claws scrabbling, and then one long, pronounced hiss. He looked to the dim light pooling through the gap at the bottom of the door, and perceived a tangle of shadows dancing just beyond. Then one of the shadows coalesced and darkened and became the end of a gnarled, bristly finger poking through the gap, and he back-pedalled away, grabbing the closest thing at hand and hurling it recklessly at the door. The glass ashtray shattered in a puff of gray and a hail of cigarette butts, and once the dust settled, both the gnarled finger and the dancing shadows were gone. He waited several interminable minutes to see if they might return, but they didn't, and so he hauled himself up to the edge of the bed, felt the mattress droop under his weight, and took stock of his situation.

He was trapped. Trapped in his childhood bedroom by a cockroach the size of a badger. *Jesus!* He tried to think the thing through, but it was just too much. After fighting his phobia for two hours straight, this was just too *goddamn* much! How the *hell* was he supposed to come to grips with the idea of a cockroach as big as God*damned*zilla? How would *anyone* deal with that? Ignore it?

Deny it? Refuse to believe that a bug could ever grow that big? Try to convince himself that it was just an insect after all, and despite its preposterous size, it was still more afraid of him than he was of it?

Bullshit! Such things were all well and good in the abstract, but good *Christ!* How big did a bug have to get before logic went out the window?

He grabbed for his pack of smokes, tongued one out, lit it and puffed away madly, but it did nothing to calm his nerves. At last, he gave up and dabbed it out on the tabletop, then he went to the closet and stripped several outgrown shirts from their hangers, taking them with him back to the edge of the bed. He pulled the biggest of the shirts over his head in order to cover his naked torso as best he could, then he wrapped another of the shirts around each of his bare feet, securing them with yet another shirt torn into strips. He would have given his left nut for his running shoes, and considerably more for a good pair of hard-soled boots, but this was better than nothing. It felt good to finally not have his feet entirely bare. He tested out his makeshift slippers with a few strides around the room, then he turned his attention to finding something he might be able to use as a weapon. Another magazine from his stash? Not likely. God*damned*zilla would shrug off a rolled-up Jugs-n-Rugs as easily as he might a feather. But what, then? This was a bedroom, not an armory. There was simply nothing around to.....

Wait! That wasn't true. There was something here after all.

He picked up the rickety old table and slammed it to the ground, shattering it to pieces, then he picked through the kindling and selected one of the table legs. It was too light and too flimsy, and one end of the thing had been broken into splinters, but just the feel of having something in his hands was infinitely better than having nothing at all.

*Just you wait and see, God*damnzilla....

He threw a jaundiced glance back to the empty can of Attack and snorted, "Probably just make the fucker mad anyway." and it was so much like what a movie hero might say that he actually drew some strength from the words. He rose to his feet and padded to the door, but though he was as bolstered as he could be and the dim rectangle of light showed no shadows, still he paused.

This whole situation was fucked. Truly and deeply fucked. As fucked as fucked could be. Somewhere in the past two hours, he'd gone from the real world to full-on Rod Serling madness. Things like this didn't happen in real life! The nest? Yeah, okay, fine. Exterminators probably came across that sort of thing all the time. But the big fucker on the dresser, and now that fuckers great-granddaddy in the hallway? Nuh uh. No way. Not a chance. The dresser-fucker, he might be able to give a pass on. *Maybe*. But God*damned*zilla was something else entirely. Bugs just didn't get that big in the real world. At least not in *this* part of the world. The jungles of South America? Who knows? Australia, maybe? Hell, *everything* in Australia was big and deadly. But bugs didn't get that big in the real world. No way. Not unless they were born under a nuclear power plant in a 50's sci-fi movie. Jesus Christ! The whole situation was just so supremely and uncategorically *fucked!*

Well, whether or not he'd been somehow dropped into someone else's nightmare, there was nothing else for it, so before he had the time to question his rashness, he took hold of the doorknob, twisted it, readied his makeshift weapon, and swung the door wide open......

There was nothing there. The hallway was empty. Anyone else might have been relieved, but not so Harold. He knew better. The thing might be gone for now, but it wasn't gone for good. Maybe it had calculated the odds of doing battle with two hundred pounds of sentient meat and retreated back to whatever dark underbelly it had come from, or maybe it was close by and watching from the shadows. But either way, it wasn't gone for good. *Hell* no. It would stay hidden just long enough for the human to let down its guard, and then it would attack. Of that, Harold was certain, but he was just as certain that there was no way on God's green Earth he would let that happen.

The hallway wasn't big, but he spent a considerable amount of time padding gingerly about and stabbing his table leg into every corner and every dark recess, even if it seemed too impossibly small to hide such a massive creature. He kicked the vacuum cleaner aside, ready to jump back lest the monster reveal itself hiding between its coils, then he probed all along the baseboards and along the ceiling tiles, just in case. Then he went into the laundry room and threw towels and dirty clothes and his mother's unmentionables in wild confusion lest the creature be taking refuge amidst the folds, but his search proved fruitless.

There was nothing there. Nothing at all.

But how could that be? There were only a limited number of places a creature that big could hide, so where the hell did God*damned*zilla go?

Even as he asked the question, he knew the answer. Surely, since mankind first climbed down from the trees and lit the world with fire, creatures of the dark had fled to their secret places. Bats to their caves. Scorpions to their rotted tree stumps. Rats into their burrows. And cockroaches..... To where had cockroaches retreated? Disgusting vermin that they were, cockroaches had gone to the one place where no other creature would ever go. They had taken refuge in the stench and filth of those early men.

The sewers. It had to be. Sewers and cockroaches went hand in hand.

He swung his crude weapon to his shoulder and padded cautiously toward the bathroom, sweeping every inch of floor and walls and ceiling all the way with wide, unblinking eyes. He paused at very threshold of the bathroom and peered into the darkness, and that was when he knew that he'd been right on the money. A sound was coming out of the blackness within, like the rustling of dried leaves on an autumn morning.

Leaning in through the doorway, he became aware of an uncertain movement in the far corner of the room; a shadowy shifting of mass as indistinct as the sound itself. He groped along the wall for the light switch and stabbed it on, then he slowly eased himself around the corner, and what he saw seized the very breath in his throat.

The shower stall was lit from within as well as without. The milky-white translucent glass door was closed, but something was casting a shadow over the bottom half of the glass. But somehow, the shadow was moving. For one insane moment, he imagined that he was watching some sort of witch's brew, roiling and bubbling away behind the glass, but the illusion didn't last long. He knew exactly what that shadow was.

They must have come up through the drain in their hundreds and thousand. Now, the thing was a seething cauldron of horror, up to height of three feet or more. The entire shower stall was alive with cockroaches!

So much mass pressed against the door that he was certain the tiny magnet holding the thing closed must surely give way. And when that eventually happened, he knew exactly what he would do. As that roiling sea poured out in a wave, he would deliver an ear-splitting shriek, he would clutch desperately at his heart, and he would collapse dead to the tile floor because it would simply be too much to take.

He watched in horrified fascination as the witch's brew boiled away, but then he saw one dark shape detach itself from the main body and begin to ascend the door. Through the milk-white opacity, he could discern little more that an abundance of narrow black legs that appeared and disappeared as they alit on the glass and then lifted off again, but behind this tangle of limbs was a distinct body, ebon black and a big as a playing card, rising away from the general mass.

The creature didn't climb purposefully, but ambled in an awkward, serpentine path, up and across the shower door from left to right. And behind it, three other shapes suddenly broke away from the main body and began to drift upward in it's wake; smaller, less distinct, but quicker. And it was only then that Harold looked to the gap between the door and the ceiling. The space separating the two was no more than six inches, but it was directly toward that opening that the shadowy quartet now made.

The idea occurred to him that if he could block that gap, the swarm would be forever trapped, but there was nothing bigger than a towel at hand. He considered retrieving the can of Attack on the off-chance that it hadn't been entirely spent and that he could turn the shower stall into his own private Auschwitz, or instead, maybe he should just grab the ElectroShag from the hallway and let the little pig eat its fill, but there was no time for either of those things. The quartet of cockroaches would reach the gap in seconds, and once they did, the word would be out and the entire horde would swarm up and over the door in a flood.

But no. It wouldn't take that long after all. As the quartet climbed higher and higher, fingers of shadows began to stretch upward from the roiling mass, then the fingers coalesced as a wave of black crested toward the gap. And with so much weight now pushing against the door, the little magnet suddenly reached its limit. It shuddered briefly, then a crack appeared all along the length of the door, and with no choice left and no weapon greater than a splintered table leg in his possession, Harold did the only thing he could. Acting on pure guttural instinct, he ran the few short steps and threw himself against the door, slamming it shut with enough force to make the thing shake in its very frame.

The effect was immediate. The shadowy quartet and the cresting wave were thrown back and swallowed up by the whole, but it didn't end there. As the glass vibrated in its frame like a tuning fork, the great mass of bodies that had been pressed against it suddenly receded in a wave. Some of the creatures undoubtedly made for a quick exit back down the drain, but the greater mass of the swarm simply swept up the back side of the stall in momentary alarm, and in that brief second that the glass was clear, Harold made his most audacious and daring move of the day. He gave the glass one more good *thump!* with the side of his fist to buy himself another second or two, and before he had a chance to second-guess his plan, he grabbed the door handle, cracked it open just wide enough to fit his pudgy arm through, and grabbed for the hot water faucet, turning it as far as it would go. A few of the quicker bugs attempted a breakout while the door was cracked open, but Harold slammed it shut again just in time to cut one in half and sever the forelimbs of two others, and then there was nothing for him to do but watch the bedlam.

The swarm reacted with the first droplets of water and flooded up all four walls in a torrent, but whenever the wave came anywhere near the top of the door, Harold pounded the glass with his fist and sent them all raining back down. Then the first wisps of steam began to rise, and utter chaos descended. The creatures clambered all over one another in a mad panic to escape the scalding water, but with Harold pounding out a constant drumbeat on the door and no other means of escape open, the water finally began to take its inevitable toll.

It was a slow process, but as the water grew hotter and the steam grew denser, the sea of black eventually started to diminish, and after an eternity that might have been counted in minutes, the last few creatures were swallowed up by the steam, and all within grew quiet. Harold let the water run on and on, and only after several more minutes went by with no discernible movement from within, he cracked the door open an inch, put a cautious eye to the gap, and uttered an audible gasp.

How so many cockroaches of such size had managed to squeeze through the grating, he hadn't a clue, but now the crumpled bodies of those behemoths blocked the drain completely, and the resultant pool of water swirling slowly about them bore the smaller corpses along in its wake. There were hundreds of them, *thousands*, ranging in size from tiny little, pill-sized bugs to fat, loathsome bastards as big as a man's hand. But there was no God*damned*zilla, nor could there ever have been. Harold knew at once that God*damned*zilla had never been a part of this horde. The bastards might be able to fit through impossibly tight spaces, but it was simply inconceivable that anything as big as a badger could have come up through this drain.

But then, why had they come? What conceivable mechanism could draw an army of cockroaches out in the open in their hundreds and thousands? A call of the wild, maybe? Had they come in answer to the death screams of the others? Was such a thing even possible? No. No way. Sure, bugs could communicate through chemical signals and the like, but it was rudimentary at best. And even if their pheromones of the dying had somehow found their way into the plumbing, the scent of death would have sent every other bug within nose-shot running the other way.

It was a coincidence, that's all. Sheer coincidence. He was just lucky that it'd happened now, when he was as mentally prepared for it as he could ever hope to be. They could just as easily have poured out in the middle of the night, or when he was on the crapper or.....or even when he was taking a shower.

This last thought sent his belly into convulsions, and he barely managed to close the shower door and get to the sink before his stomach lurched. He gripped the edge of the counter and wretched, and when he turned on the tap to wash the worst of it away, the sight of it circling the drain made him vomit again. And again. And then again.

When he simply had no more to give and his stomach had at last began to settle, he splashed a handful of water in his face, used more to rinse the bitterness from his mouth, and finally lifted his chin to look at himself in the mirror. The eyes staring back were half-lidded and rimmed with red, the cheeks were drawn and heavily-lined, and the flesh was the colour of death. But behind it all was a grim self-satisfaction. This night's work had taken its toll, but he'd made it. He'd faced the worst of his fears in a way that few men would ever be called to do, and he'd survived. *Hell* no. He hadn't just survived, he'd *won!*

"Gotcha, you dirty little bastards," he said into the mirror, loving the way his voice sounded all raw and gravelly, "Got the whole mother-fucking lot of you….."

He threw a quick glance toward the shower door, but he simply didn't have enough left in the tank to see to those thousands of corpses right now. That particular horror would have to wait for a new day. In fact, maybe he'd just leave the cleaning-up to the old fogeys. Let them get just a little taste of what he'd been through, and then let them try to live with the nightmares.

He took one last look in the mirror and shared a sneer with himself, then he turned and stepped out into the hallway, only to come to an abrupt halt.

God*damned*zilla sat in the precise center of the hallway, reared back on its haunches and stabbing a single finger-sized forelimb directly at the man.

This time, there was no hesitation. After everything he'd been through, Harold was beyond anything approaching rational thought. He charged at the monster in great, heavy strides, and brought his weapon down in a great sweeping arc that caught the creature dead center across the back. But the carapace was thick and the table leg flimsy, and the blow bounced off as if it'd struck iron. The creature reared back and hissed again, and as Harold took another swing, it actually reached out with its horrible thorny legs and grabbed hold of the very end of the table leg. It could never hope to win the tug-o'-war, but it held on long enough for a clumsy backswing to carry it high up into the air, and Harold had to leap to the side to keep it from landing on him.

The thing hit the ground with a discernible *thud!* and reared back with a hiss, then it broke into a skittering run, tearing back down the hallway like an angry bull. Harold was forced into a retreat, but he didn't run, and he didn't stop fighting. He backed away one faltering step at a time and swung his useless weapon for all he was worth, but the massive creature shrugged off each and every blow.

At last, he felt the laundry room door at his back and knew that he could go no farther. In desperation then, he spun the weapon around so that the splintered ends were facing downward, and he threw all of prodigious weight behind one desperate plunge. And though the carapace was far too thick to be pierced by such a flimsy weapon, the table leg rode down the rounded dome and skidded off the edge of the thing, and as if it had been the most unerring shot in the world, it happened to catch the creature in the exact center of its massive, tear-shaped head. The splintered end of the table leg skewered the monster right between its big compound eyes, came out somewhere behind its snapping mouth, and didn't stop until it buried itself in the deep pile of the carpeting.

Still, the thing thrashed and twisted and skittered about on its ugly, fat legs, but Harold kept it pinned to the spot, leaning all of his weight on the thing keeping it in place. And even as he wondered how he could possibly kill such a monster that could survive a spear through its head, he knew that there was only one thing he could do.

He brought up his foot and stomped it down directly on the creature's back with a horrible *craack!*, and when he saw a hairline fracture appear along the length of the carapace, he stomped again.

And again.

And again.

A sickly blue gore sprayed in every direction, painting the walls, puddling on the floor and soaking through the old shirt wrapped around his foot, but Harold was beyond caring. He ignored it all and kept stomping until there was nothing left to stomp. At last, he felt the unforgiving floor under his foot and forced himself to stop, and then and only then did he see what he had done.

The major portion of the creature's body had vanished. Only the head and legs remained, attached by strings of sinew to bits of goo and shards of carapace pasted into the carpet. But even so, and even with the spear of the table leg still pinning the bodiless head to the floor, the creature was not yet done. A single forelimb rose up out of the mess and aimed itself right at him. But then it faltered, palsied, and dropped back down to the puddle of mire, and the creature expelled the last of its life in one last prolonged hiss.

For a mind already bent to the breaking point, it was too much. Suddenly, it was all Harold could do to pull his foot free from the gore with a horrible *shluuck!* and shuffle the few feet to his bedroom, dragging a trail of offal behind. He rounded the corner out of sheer muscle memory, and when he felt his shin bark up against the edge of the bed, he collapsed forward and let the mattress catch him.

Then, there was nothing. Only the dark, silent stupor of a dead, dreamless sleep.

****

He became aware as consciousness returned by slow degrees. Sometime during the night, his sleep had become fitful and filled with nightmares, and every last one of them were of the skittering things.

His first conscious thought was that of a sharp pain behind his eyes and an incessant chatter from somewhere inside his head, and as the vestiges of a host of nightmares began to dissipate, he realized that they hadn't been nightmares at all. They were memories. All of those horrible things had actually happened, after all.

Jesus Lord-a'Mighty, no wonder his skull felt like it was coming apart. All of that shit had actually happened. The nest, the shower, God*damned*zilla.....all of it. Every little bit of that living Hell had actually happened!

He became suddenly aware of a dull aching in his legs and arms and all up his back, and no wonder. But it wasn't anything a few cold beers and a trip through the old folks' medicine cabinet couldn't fix. Hell, maybe he'd even pry open one of old Jimmy Stanton's windows next door and help himself to the old fart's personal stash. It wouldn't be the first time, and good *Christ!* He'd been through Hell and back, so if there was ever a man deserving of a little self-indulgence.....

He wondered how long he'd been asleep, but it was simply too much work to bring up his wristwatch and pry his eyes open. Well, no matter. If the old fogeys weren't home by now, they would be soon enough. And if no one came downstairs right away, that was okay too. Eventually, the old lady would bring down a load of laundry, and she'd see the surprise waiting for her in the hallway. She'd scream, and the old man would waddle down to find out what the ruckus was about, and then he'd see it too. And just when they thought they'd seen the worst of it, Harold would come out and usher them both into the bathroom and leave them there, cowering in fear.

A sneer crept across his lips, and he turned his attention to listening for sounds from above. If they were home, he'd hear footsteps. Floorboards creaking. Water running. Toilet flushing. But there was nothing. All he could hear was the background chatter inside his own aching head.

Christ, he'd been on benders before, but this was something else. His skull felt like it was filled with lava. If only he could get upstairs to that pharmacy of meds in the old folks' bathroom, sure as shit he'd be able to put himself right. But getting there would be like walking that last green mile. Hell, if he couldn't summon the energy to check his own wristwatch, how was he ever going to haul his ass upstairs?

He tried again to bring up his arm, and this time he really tried. He sent out the appropriate commands and felt his muscles flex, but he was simply too sore and too weak to perform even that simple task. It was too much, after all. Hell, if he was that worn out, maybe he'd just stay right there in bed until the rapture. But no sooner had he come to that decision than he became aware of an oddly tingling sensation in his limbs. Blood rushing back? Sensations returning? Maybe, but this wasn't the usual pins and needles. It was more of an indistinct pressure; a heaviness, even. And there was something else, too. The chattering in his head was growing in intensity, gaining in volume with every thundering beat of his heart. It was almost as if.....

He snapped his eyes open in a sudden fit of panic, but all he could see at first was the bare bulb hanging over his head. He tried to sit up, but though he could feel his muscles respond, his body didn't move. Then the chattering grew louder and the heaviness grew more pronounced, and he craned his head up off of the bed to see what he knew he would see.

His entire body was covered in cockroaches. Big, small and everywhere in-between, they covered his entire body from his toes to his throat, and with such thickness that he couldn't move a muscle under their weight. Then a deeper heaviness near his feet had him craning his neck even farther, and he watched as a single limb, as white as snow and as wide around as a man's arm, poked up over the edge of the mattress. It groped drunkenly around at first, then that one limb was joined by a second, and a third and fourth, and at last, a giant head appeared over the edge.

The head was the size of a basketball, but the body that followed behind simply defied logic. The bed creaked and groaned as the monstrous creature clambered its way up, then it flopped down and spread out across the entire mattress, pinning the man from feet to chest.

At last, the thing growled a hiss, and the background chatter abruptly stopped. It reached out a thick, muscular forelimb and tapped it on the man's protruding belly, and even in his addled state, Harold knew exactly what it was doing. It was communicating with the others. Giving them orders.

It was telling them to feed.

****

Old Jimmy Stanton awoke with a start, and in that blurred infinity between dreams and wakefulness, he thought he'd heard something. A scream, it sounded like, but there was nothing now. Whatever it had been was shut off as quickly as it'd started. Or maybe there was never anything there to begin with.

He bunched the pillow under his head, and without giving the matter another thought, he fell back into a deep, blissful sleep.

The End

Thank you very much for reading Jitters. If you enjoyed it, please consider posting a review on Amazon. If you would like to see more of Ken Stark's work, visit his Amazon page at

https://www.amazon.com/Ken-Stark/e/B01D911QC2

or drop in on the author's website at

https://www.kenstark.ca

For now, please enjoy this excerpt from the author's latest release, Arcadia Falls:

Arcadia Falls

by Ken Stark

PROLOGUE

tap! tap! tap!

tap! tap! tap!

He scraped up a fresh handful of pebbles and picked out the best of the lot, then he took careful aim at the boulder in the middle of the river and let them fly, one after another after another. They arced gracefully out over the water, striking the face of the boulder with a gentle *tap! tap! tap!,* and the cute little girl with the big brown eyes and the face full of freckles giggled.

He scraped up another handful and picked out the best of the lot, and this time, he handed them to the girl. She watched the pebbles tumble into her tiny little hand as if they were the shiniest of jewels, and then she smiled at him, and he felt his heart flutter.

The first pebble landed short and disappeared with a *bloop!*, and the girl giggled as the river carried away the ripples. So he shared with her his secrets about the overhand throw and the special flick of the wrist, and she tried again, and this time, the pebble *blooped!* into the water just inches shy of the target. On the third try, the pebble hit the boulder square on the face, so they both cheered and laughed and high-fived, and then there was that one single lifetime of seconds when they just sat there and looked into each other's eyes.

He scraped up another handful and picked out the best of lot, and after they'd all tumbled into the cute little girl's hand, he gave her one more that he'd kept separate. It was the prettiest pebble in the world, he told her, because it had the same flecks of gold that she had in her eyes, and then he watched a smile swell those beautiful freckled cheeks as she tucked that most special of jewels carefully away in a pocket.

tap! tap! tap!

tap! tap! tap!

Before long, the cute little girl with the big brown eyes and the face full of freckles was as good as he, and they both scraped up handful after handful, tossing them at the boulder in the middle of the river with a steady *tap! tap! tap!* But then the riverbank gave way, and the girl slipped into the water, and though he grabbed for her again and again, her tiny little hand stayed always just desperately out of reach. She called out his name over and over, even as she floated away, but the river was swift, and it soon carried her into its strongest currents. And when she finally floated far enough away that he couldn't hear her anymore or see her anymore, he sat back down, scooped up another handful of pebbles, picked out the best of the lot, and resumed throwing them at the boulder, one after another after another.

tap! tap! tap!

tap! tap! tap!

He sat bolt upright in bed, his face dripping with sweat. He took a moment to let the awful images fade away, then he plucked his wet pajama top away from his skin and breathed a sigh of relief.

A dream.....It was just a dream.....

He laid back down to find his pillow wet with sweat, so he flipped it over and settled back in, pulling the covers close around his neck. Suddenly, he was shivering, and he knew the reason why. Even in the dead of winter, his dad always turned the thermostat down at night. It always seemed to him a ridiculous way to save a few pennies, but he'd already heard the whole 'I don't pay to heat the whole neighbourhood' lecture more times than he cared to remember, so even shivering in bed with hailstones pattering against the window, it just wasn't worth tiptoeing out to try to sneak the needle back up a few degrees.

Well, maybe it wasn't all bad news after all. If the storm kept up all night, maybe they'd even cancel school tomorrow. Sure, his dad would make him shovel the driveway, but that was a small price to pay for…..

Wait a second….. That's not right…..

A flood of recent memories washed through his mind and swept away the last images of half-remembered nightmares. He and his buddies in the park. An ice cream truck playing its too-loud music. Bigger kids, hogging the place with their frisbees and their skateboards.

But that was just yesterday. It wasn't winter, it was summer, so what the…..

It was the nightmare, that's what it was. The nightmare that'd made him sweat through his pajamas and left the middle of the bed all cold and wet enough to make him shiver. That stupid little-boy nightmare he couldn't even remember anymore. *Stupid little-boy nightmares…..*he thought, and suddenly he couldn't wait to be grown up so he'd never have nightmares again.

He rolled onto his stomach and let his head sink into his pillow, and as he drifted back through the nebulous world between reality and dreams, he heard it again.

tap! tap! tap!

tap! tap! tap!

It *was* hail. Hail pelting against the window. But it *couldn't* be hail. It wasn't winter, it was summer. And besides, the tapping was too regular, too deliberate. For all the world, it sounded like someone was standing just outside, tapping out a message in Morse code. Could it be one of his friends, maybe? Someone paying him a late-night visit? No, not a chance. No one he knew would be caught *dead* wandering the streets at night.

He climbed out of bed and padded across to the window, then he stopped just short and listened again.

tap! tap! tap!

tap! tap! tap!

Okay, someone was *definitely* outside. No doubt about it, somebody was standing on the other side of the window, tapping on the glass. He had the sudden idea that it might be a burglar, but what kind of burglar knocked to get in? No, this had to be someone he knew. One of his friends, not wanting to wake the whole house. But in the middle of the night? Well, if one of his friends was *that* desperate, there was only one thing he could do. His parents wouldn't like it, but friends help friends, no matter what. And so, the entire matter settled at last, he reached for the curtains and threw them open.....
.....and his blood turned to ice.

This wasn't a friend. This wasn't even someone in a Hamburglar mask trying to break in. This was….. This was….. *Oh, dear sweet Jesus*.....

He had the briefest glimpse of ugly red eyes, then the thing on the other side came suddenly to life and began skipping and dancing across the window from one side to the other and back again. Then it reared back and began to throw itself bodily at the window, and for one horrible moment, he was sure that the glass would break. And yet, he made no move to run. Through it all, his own terror kept him rooted to the spot, and it was all he could do to suck in a breath, release it in a silent whimper, and watch the unimaginable *thing* flail away on the opposite side of the glass.

At last, after an eternity, the sounds stopped and the thing held perfectly still. It peered in at him across a space of inches, and then, another eternity later, it sank slowly out of view and all he could see beyond the window was a deep, fathomless night. And even as he stood there, unable to move, unable to cry out and unable to make sense of anything he'd just seen, a new sound erupted from out of nowhere.

It was a scream. A child's scream. It went on and on and on, filling the fathomless night. And then came the pounding of feet across the ceiling and frantic little bursts of shouting from above, so he knew he hadn't imagined it. The scream had awoken his parents, and in another few seconds, the rest of the neighbourhood would be awake too. He kept watch at the window for the lights that were sure to come on all up and down the street, and he watched for the dozens of neighbours who would emerge from their homes and come and join him in his fear so that he could tell them of the monster he'd seen right outside his window, but they didn't come. Not a single neighbour emerged. Not a single light went on.

Eventually, the feet stopped pounding, and then the frantic little bursts of shouting stopped, too. And once the whole of the night grew as still and silent as a graveyard, he uprooted himself from the spot, drew the curtains closed, and padded back to his bed. He climbed between sheets still moist with sweat and laid his head on a cold, damp pillow, and by the time he began to drift back to sleep, he had already convinced himself that it must have been just another dream after all. Just a dream within a dream.

All that we see or seem.....

The words he barely knew drifted through his wearied mind and eventually faded away into nothingness. His last conscious thought was of a cute little girl with big brown eyes and a face full of freckles, but then she faded away too. And as sleep came to reclaim him, he became distantly aware of one last sound. It was the sound of a baby crying, far, far away.

A single heartbeat later, that too was silenced, and he fell into a deep, restless sleep.

www.ingramcontent.com/pod-product-compliance
Lightning Source LLC
Chambersburg PA
CBHW071222130626
46555CB00004B/1801